D1107572

Sleeping Beauty

and other fairytales

Sleeping Beauty
and other fairytales

Retold by Stephanie Laslett

‖ •PARRAGON• ‖

A Parragon Book

Published by
Parragon Publishing,
Queen Street House, 4 Queen Street,
Bath BA1 1HE

Produced by
The Templar Company plc,
Pippbrook Mill, London Road, Dorking,
Surrey RH4 1JE

Printed and bound in China.
ISBN 0 75253 122 0

Contents

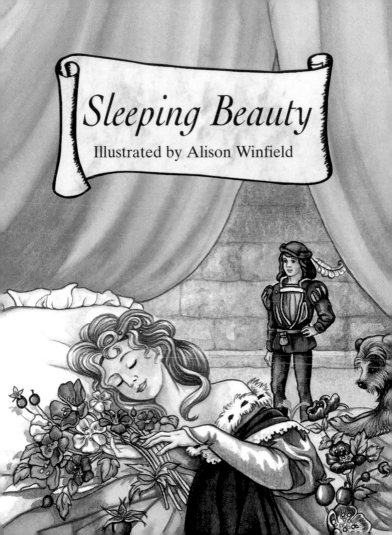

Sleeping Beauty

Illustrated by Alison Winfield

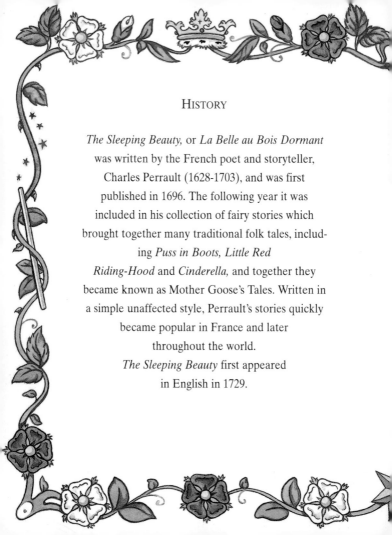

HISTORY

The Sleeping Beauty, or *La Belle au Bois Dormant*
was written by the French poet and storyteller,
Charles Perrault (1628-1703), and was first
published in 1696. The following year it was
included in his collection of fairy stories which
brought together many traditional folk tales, includ-
ing *Puss in Boots, Little Red
Riding-Hood* and *Cinderella,* and together they
became known as Mother Goose's Tales. Written in
a simple unaffected style, Perrault's stories quickly
became popular in France and later
throughout the world.
The Sleeping Beauty first appeared
in English in 1729.

Once upon a time there was a King and Queen. They lived in a fine Palace but lacked the one thing that would bring them happiness — a child of their own.

At last, however, the Queen had a daughter. Great was their joy as they held the Baby Princess. Her skin was as soft and as sweet as rose petals and so the Queen decided to name her Briar-Rose.

The day of the Princess's Christening dawned fair and bright and everyone prepared to celebrate the

special occasion. In
those long-ago days it
was the custom to
invite all the fairies in

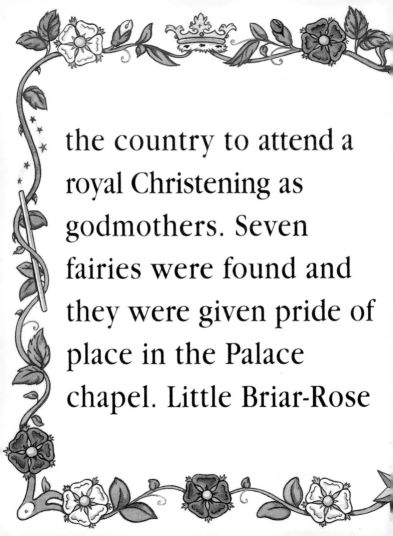

the country to attend a royal Christening as godmothers. Seven fairies were found and they were given pride of place in the Palace chapel. Little Briar-Rose

gurgled happily in her mother's arms and all agreed she was the most beautiful baby they had ever seen.

After the Christening, the King and Queen and

their guests returned to the Palace for a great feast. The hall was decked with silk ribbons and garlands of flowers. The court musicians played up in the balcony and all was joy and laughter. The table was laid with the richest food and the finest wine that money could buy. As guests of honour, each fairy had a gleaming gold plate set all around with sparkling precious jewels and their wine goblets were solid silver.

"Good health!" and
"Every happiness!"
cried the company, as

they held their drinks
high and toasted the
baby Princess.

Suddenly there was a resounding crash and the old oak door was flung open. All merriment ceased as heads turned to greet the new arrival. There on the threshold, in the bright light of the flaming torches, stood a wizened old woman. With a gasp, the Queen recognised her as a fairy who had not been seen for many, many years.

The ancient fairy
stamped her bent stick
on the floor three times.

"Why was I not invited to the Christening feast?" she demanded in a harsh, rasping voice. "Old I may be but am I to be forgotten for ever?" Hastily, the Queen tried

to calm her.

"Many years have passed since you were last seen," she explained. "Sad to say, we thought you were dead."

The fairy was very angry.

"I am not dead. I am as alive as the Princess Briar-Rose lying asleep in her cradle," and the old woman pointed a gnarled finger at the baby.

The Queen shivered. A cold chill settled over her heart and she was filled with foreboding.

"Come," she said, taking the old woman's arm. "Come and join our celebrations." Slowly the crone hobbled to a seat at the end of the table and sat down. To her anger, she could see there were only seven gold dishes and seven silver goblets and the old fairy had to make do with an ordinary pewter plate and cup.

She was furious. Loudly she grumbled as the guests made merry.

When the feast was ended it was time for the fairies to give their gifts to the Princess.

They stood in a circle
around the smiling baby.

First, the youngest fairy
gave her the gift of beauty.

Then the next wished
that she should be
wonderfully wise; the
third, that she should
be as graceful as a
swan; the fourth, that
she should dance like

an angel; the fifth, that she should sing like a nightingale; and the sixth, that she should play exquisite music.

Just then, the old fairy broke into the circle.

Shaking with rage, she bent over the cradle.

"Yes, my pretty, you shall have a gift from me. When you are fifteen you will prick your finger on a spindle — and die!"

"No, no!" cried the King and Queen.

At this all the company began to weep and wail. Then the seventh fairy spoke. "I have not yet made my wish. I will try to help the Princess but I have no power to undo entirely what my elder has done. Instead

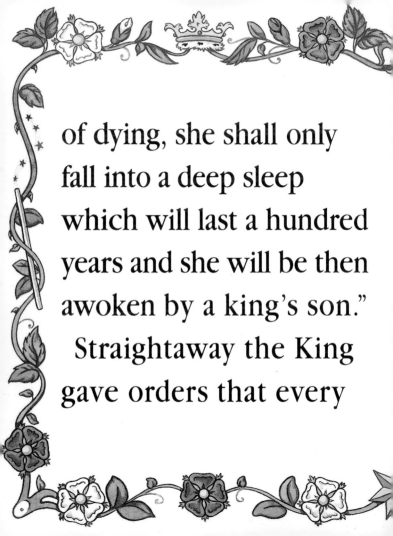

of dying, she shall only
fall into a deep sleep
which will last a hundred
years and she will be then
awoken by a king's son."
   Straightaway the King
gave orders that every

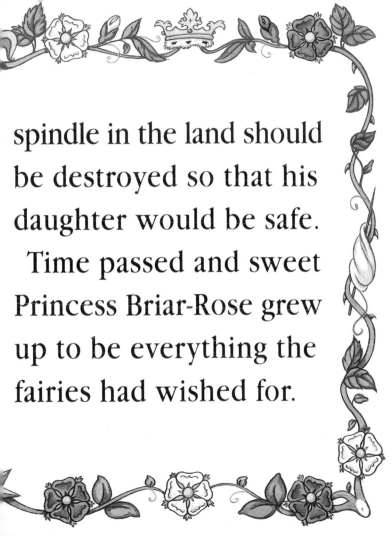

spindle in the land should be destroyed so that his daughter would be safe.

Time passed and sweet Princess Briar-Rose grew up to be everything the fairies had wished for.

She sang happily all day long and gave great joy to the King and Queen.

About fifteen years had gone by since the Royal Christening and one day the young Princess was exploring the palace. She knew most of the long passages and staircases by heart but as she turned a corner in the

west wing she saw a
little doorway she had
never noticed before.
Behind the door was a
narrow winding staircase
which led her up and
up to the very top of a

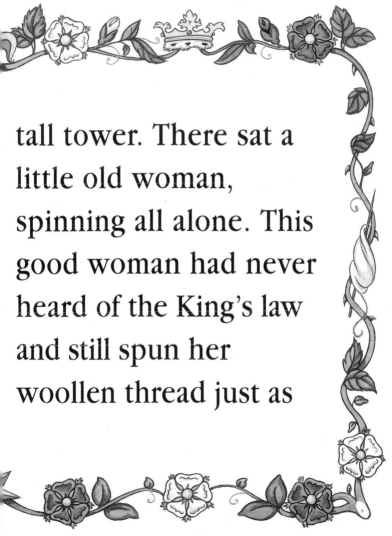

tall tower. There sat a
little old woman,
spinning all alone. This
good woman had never
heard of the King's law
and still spun her
woollen thread just as

her mother had taught her, using a spindle.

"What are you doing there, goody?" said the Princess.

"I am spinning, my pretty child," said the old woman, who did not know who she was.

"Oh, please let me see!" said the Princess. "This is very pretty; how do you do it? May I have a go?"

But as soon as she took the spindle the needle pricked her finger, and she fell down in a swoon.

The good old woman

cried out for help and
people came rushing
from every direction.

They tried all they could
to wake her up, but no-
one could rouse her.

Then the King remembered the old fairy's wish and knew that he was powerless. His only daughter, the Princess Briar-Rose, would now stay fast asleep for a hundred long years.

He ordered that she should be carried to the finest room in his palace, and laid upon a bed all embroidered with gold and silver.

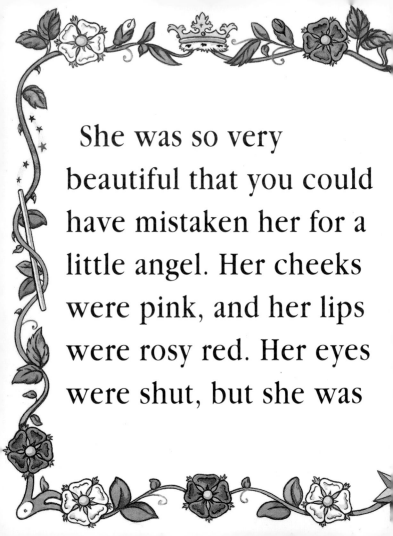

She was so very beautiful that you could have mistaken her for a little angel. Her cheeks were pink, and her lips were rosy red. Her eyes were shut, but she was

heard to breathe softly,
which satisfied those
about her that she was
not dead. The King
ordered that they should
not disturb her, but let
her sleep quietly till her

hour of awaking was
come.

When the good seventh
fairy heard the news she
came to the palace
immediately.

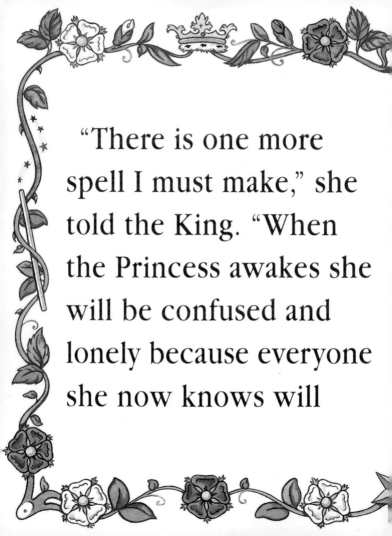

"There is one more spell I must make," she told the King. "When the Princess awakes she will be confused and lonely because everyone she now knows will have died. So I will put every other living thing in the palace into a deep sleep so they will all wake together in one hundred years' time."

The fairy tapped her

wand on everyone in the
palace; the King and the
Queen, the Maids of
Honour, the Ladies of the

Bedchamber, the fine
gentlemen, officers,
stewards, cooks, maids,
undercooks, scullions,

guards, footmen and pages. Then she tapped all the horses in the stables, the hunting dogs in the courtyard, the white doves in the dove cot and she didn't forget

pretty little Mopsey, the
Princess's spaniel, who
lay still and quiet beside
her on the bed.

Immediately they all fell
asleep and a deep silence
crept over the palace.

In an instant there grew
around the castle a hedge
of trees, great and small,
with thorns, bushes and

brambles, all twining
one within another, that
neither man nor beast
could pass through.

All that could be seen
was the very top of the
palace towers.

And so a hundred years passed by. Inside the thick thorn hedge nothing stirred.

One day a young Prince came hunting close by. He was greatly

puzzled to see the white turrets of the palace rising from a thick wood.

"Oh, that is a ruinous old castle, haunted by ghosts," said one of the huntsmen.

"That is where all the wizards and witches meet," said another.

Most agreed that an ogre lived there, and that this beast was the only one to have the power to pass through the tangled wood.

The Prince stared at the hedge, not knowing what to believe, when an aged countryman spoke out. "May it please Your Royal Highness, it is now about fifty years

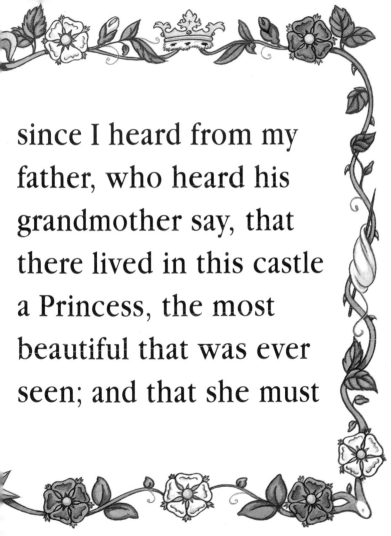

since I heard from my
father, who heard his
grandmother say, that
there lived in this castle
a Princess, the most
beautiful that was ever
seen; and that she must

sleep there for a hundred years, until she should be awakened by a Prince."

The Prince felt strangely drawn towards the tall towers, and without a moment's hesitation, he stepped into the thick thorn hedge.

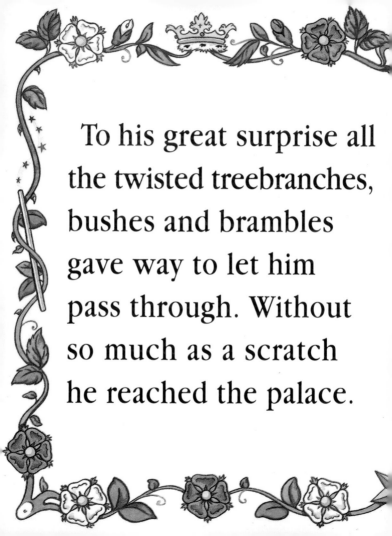

To his great surprise all the twisted treebranches, bushes and brambles gave way to let him pass through. Without so much as a scratch he reached the palace.

But none of his people could follow him because the trees closed again behind the Prince blocking their path.

As he stepped clear of the hedge he caught his

his breath. A frightening silence hung over everything. Not a bird sang, not a dog barked, not a cat mewed, not a child chattered. The brave young Prince walked

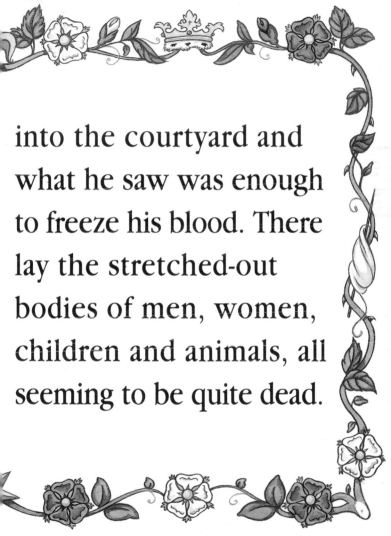

into the courtyard and
what he saw was enough
to freeze his blood. There
lay the stretched-out
bodies of men, women,
children and animals, all
seeming to be quite dead.

But when he had summoned up enough courage to look closer, he could tell by their ruby red lips that they were only fast asleep.

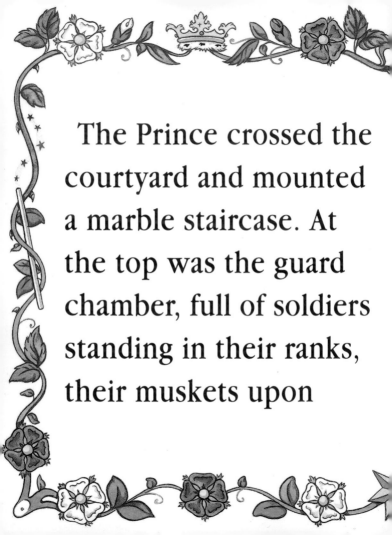

The Prince crossed the courtyard and mounted a marble staircase. At the top was the guard chamber, full of soldiers standing in their ranks, their muskets upon

their shoulders, all
snoring loudly.

Quickly he ran through
room after room, each
one full of gentlemen and
ladies. Some were
standing, others were

sitting but all of them
were fast asleep. At last
he arrived at a chamber
all gilded with gold and

there, lying on the bed,
was the Princess. The
Prince had never seen
such a beautiful

sight in all his life and instantly he fell in love. He leant over the bed and softly kissed her.

Now the enchantment had come to an end, and outside the window the white doves in the dove-cot began to sing.

Slowly the Princess awoke. She looked at him with tender eyes.

"Is it you, my Prince?" she said. "I have waited such a long time for you to find me."

The Prince, charmed by the Princess's sweet

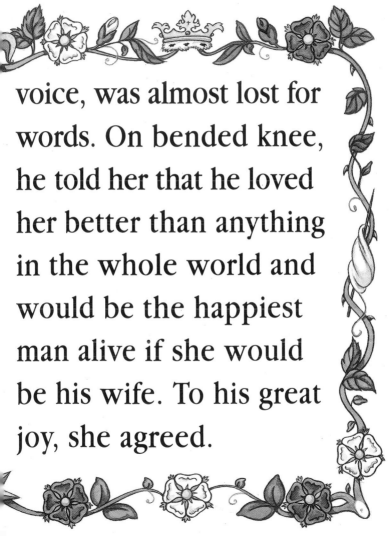

voice, was almost lost for words. On bended knee, he told her that he loved her better than anything in the whole world and would be the happiest man alive if she would be his wife. To his great joy, she agreed.

There was much rejoicing in the palace when it was heard that Princess Briar-Rose was alive and happy.

From a high balcony, golden trumpets rang out and the news of the Royal Wedding was announced. Cheers filled the air as the King and Queen welcomed the Prince and kissed

their new-found daughter.
And loud were the
cheers in the Great Hall
that day as courtiers
and servants alike ate
their first meal for a
hundred years and
outside in the courtyard

the dogs chased their tails with excitement. So the Sleeping Beauty and her Prince were married amidst great joy and after the wedding, lived happily evermore.

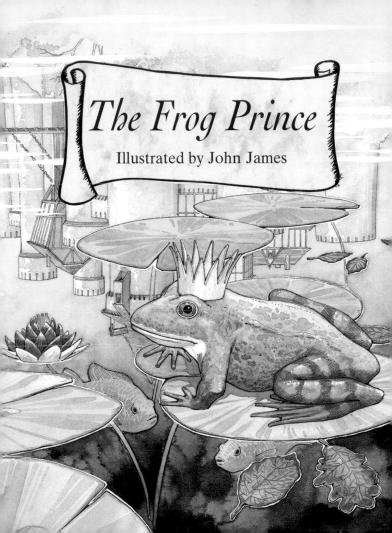

The Frog Prince

Illustrated by John James

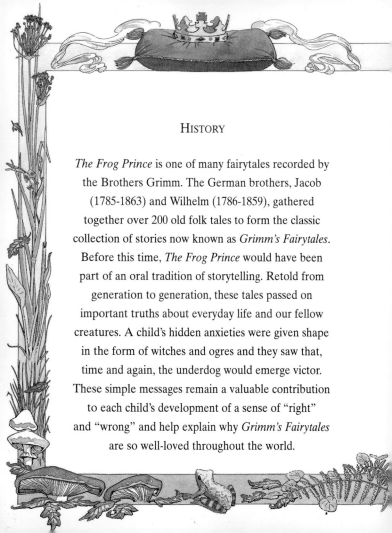

HISTORY

The Frog Prince is one of many fairytales recorded by
the Brothers Grimm. The German brothers, Jacob
(1785-1863) and Wilhelm (1786-1859), gathered
together over 200 old folk tales to form the classic
collection of stories now known as *Grimm's Fairytales*.
Before this time, *The Frog Prince* would have been
part of an oral tradition of storytelling. Retold from
generation to generation, these tales passed on
important truths about everyday life and our fellow
creatures. A child's hidden anxieties were given shape
in the form of witches and ogres and they saw that,
time and again, the underdog would emerge victor.
These simple messages remain a valuable contribution
to each child's development of a sense of "right"
and "wrong" and help explain why *Grimm's Fairytales*
are so well-loved throughout the world.

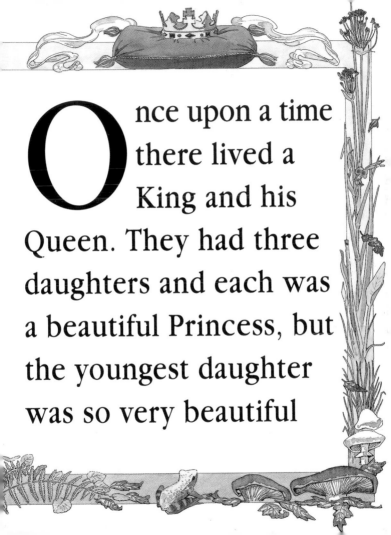

Once upon a time there lived a King and his Queen. They had three daughters and each was a beautiful Princess, but the youngest daughter was so very beautiful that she brought joy to the heart of everyone who laid eyes on her. She had long gold-red hair, shining green eyes and her laughter was like the tinkling of silver fairy bells.

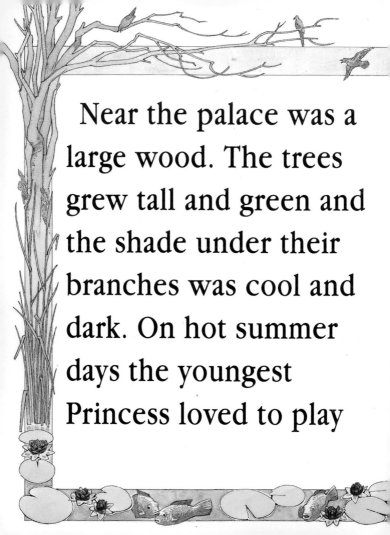

Near the palace was a large wood. The trees grew tall and green and the shade under their branches was cool and dark. On hot summer days the youngest Princess loved to play here, chasing dappled sunbeams and dreaming secret dreams.

On one such day the sun shone down from a cloudless sky and not a breath of air stirred in the Palace grounds.

The King and Queen and the three lovely Princesses drowsed behind drawn curtains, their silk fans fluttering lazily in their hands.

The youngest Princess longed for the cool shade of the wood. Quietly she slipped from the room, ran across the meadow and into the welcome shade of the beech trees. She

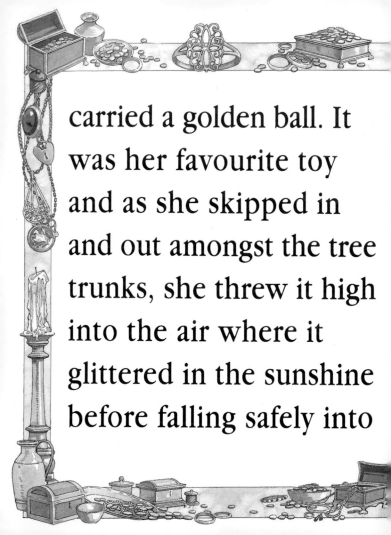

carried a golden ball. It was her favourite toy and as she skipped in and out amongst the tree trunks, she threw it high into the air where it glittered in the sunshine before falling safely into

her small hands.

Soon she reached an open glade deep in the heart of the wood. In the middle of the clearing was a beautiful fountain and the splashing of the sparkling water was like

music to her ears. With
a merry laugh, she threw
her ball high into the air.
She stretched out her
arms to catch but it
slipped through her
fingers, rolled over the
ground and splash! fell

into the fountain pool.
Slowly it sank beneath
the water and dropped
out of sight.

With a cry of dismay,
the young Princess
knelt down and peered
into the water. But the

pool was very deep and
her ball was lost.
Heartbroken, the little

Princess began to weep.
Tears fell from her eyes
into the still, grey water.

With each tear drop,
trembling ripples spread
out across the pool.
Suddenly, the Princess
heard a small voice.
  "Oh, Princess, why do
you weep so sadly?"
  Startled, she looked all

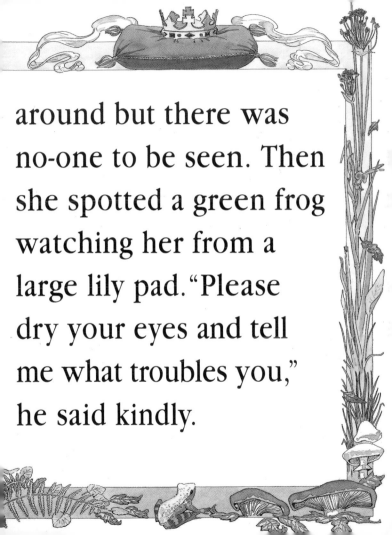

around but there was no-one to be seen. Then she spotted a green frog watching her from a large lily pad. "Please dry your eyes and tell me what troubles you," he said kindly.

"Oh, Frog," she sighed. "I am sad because I have lost my golden ball. It fell into the pool and now it is gone for ever."

The little Princess's lip quivered and she began to cry again.

"Hush, now," said the Frog. "I may be able to help but if I do this for you, then you must do something for me."

The Princess clasped
her hands. "If I could
only have my ball again
I would give you all my
fine clothes, my jewels
and everything that I have
in the world," she cried.
"I do not want your

clothes or your jewels," said the Frog, "but let me eat from your own golden plate and let me sleep in your own golden bed and then I will promise to fetch your golden ball."

The Princess thought for a moment. "What nonsense this silly frog is talking," she said to herself. "He will never be able to leave this pool on his own, so I will pretend to agree to his

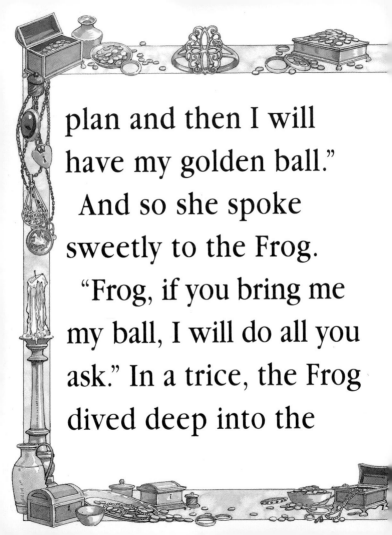

plan and then I will have my golden ball."

And so she spoke sweetly to the Frog.

"Frog, if you bring me my ball, I will do all you ask." In a trice, the Frog dived deep into the

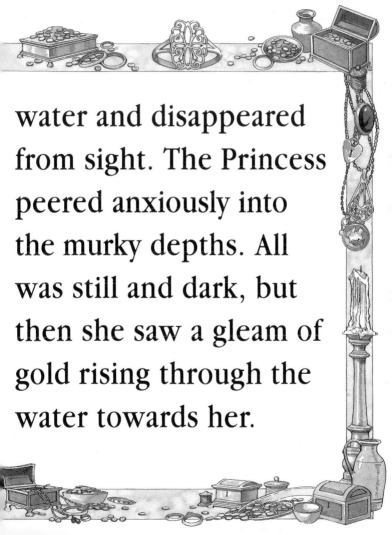

water and disappeared
from sight. The Princess
peered anxiously into
the murky depths. All
was still and dark, but
then she saw a gleam of
gold rising through the
water towards her.

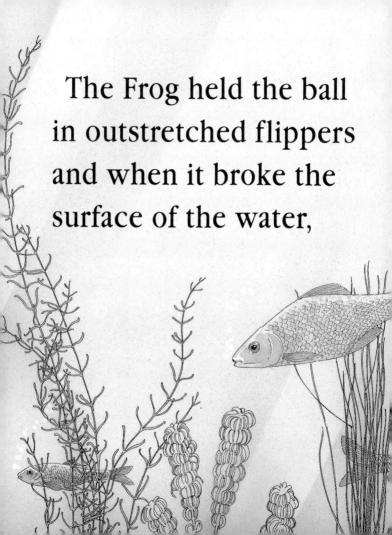

The Frog held the ball
in outstretched flippers
and when it broke the
surface of the water,

sunlight glanced off the
shining globe and bright
beams of light lit up the
woodland glade.

Overjoyed, the Princess took her ball from the Frog and, without a second thought, ran for home as fast as she could.

"Stop, stop!" the Frog called after her. "You promised to take me with you," but, with red hair flying and a merry laugh, she was gone.

Next day the Princess had forgotten all about the Frog. She sat down for dinner at the Palace with her father, her

mother, her two sisters
and all the courtiers.
But as she raised her

first spoonful of soup to
her mouth she heard a
strange noise outside.

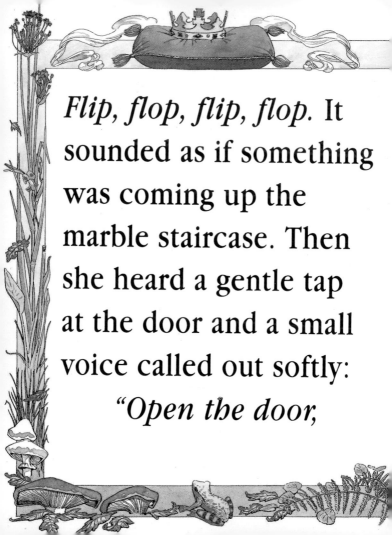

Flip, flop, flip, flop. It sounded as if something was coming up the marble staircase. Then she heard a gentle tap at the door and a small voice called out softly:

"Open the door,

my Princess dear.
Open the door
to your true love here!
And remember
the words that
you and I said,
by the fountain cool,in
the greenwood shade."

The little Princess ran to the door and there squatted the Frog. His round eyes bulged and his green skin glistened. The Princess slammed the door and hurried back to her seat.

The King saw that she was pale and trembling. "What is the matter, little daughter? Has an ogre come to call?" he joked.

With tears in her eyes, she recounted all that had happened the day before in the wood.

"My golden ball fell into the fountain pool and a nasty green Frog returned it safely to me.

I promised him that he could come and live with me here but I hoped he would never be able to leave the pool and find me. Now he is outside the door and wants to come in!"

As she finished talking,
she heard another gentle
tap at the door.

"Open the door,
my Princess dear.
Open the door
to your true love here!
And remember

*the words that
you and I said,
by the fountain cool, in
the greenwood shade.*"
The King looked at the
Princess gravely. "You
made a promise, my
little daughter, and now

you must keep your word. Let the Frog enter."

The Princess walked back to the door with a heavy heart. Opening it wide, she stood to one side and the Frog hopped over the threshold.

Her sisters, the Queen
and the Ladies-in-Waiting
gasped in horror, for
the Frog was very ugly.

They all gathered their
skirts about them and
shrank back as the little
creature passed by.

Flip, flop, flip, flop.
With everyone's eyes
upon him, the Frog
hopped the whole length
of the dining hall
leaving a long trail of
damp patches. He
headed straight for the

youngest Princess's
chair and reluctantly,
she followed behind.
Nobody stirred. When
he reached her place at
the table the Frog
stopped and looked up
at her golden chair.

"Please lift me up so I can sit beside you," he croaked. The Princess wrinkled her beautiful nose in disgust.

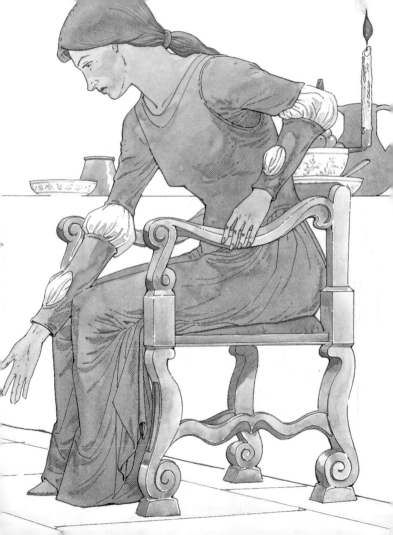

"I can't touch you, you horrid Frog," she cried. Her father spoke sternly. "You must do as he bids. A promise is a promise." With a shiver, she wrapped her soft white fingers around his fat belly and lifted him on to the table.

"Please push your plate nearer to me," said the Frog. "I want to be able to share your food."

The Queen moaned. "My fan! Fetch my fan!"

she wailed, and indeed showed every sign of fainting clean away. The two older Princesses could watch no longer and, with a muffled squeak, buried their faces in their napkins.

Slowly, the youngest Princess pushed her plate towards the Frog. With long, webbed fingers he picked delicately at the dainty morsels. From time to time a long tongue darted from his mouth

and caught a tasty titbit. Frozen with disgust, the whole court watched his every move. After a while, the Frog leant back and patted his stomach.

"I can eat no more," he confessed to the Princess.

"Now I am tired. Please carry me upstairs. I want to sleep on your bed."

The Queen groaned softly from behind her fan. The Princesses buried their faces ever deeper into their napkins. But the little Princess could not break her word.

The courtiers watched open-mouthed as she carried the Frog from the hall and climbed the marble stairs

"Please let me lie upon your silken pillow," said the Frog.

"No, no, no!" cried the wretched Princess, stamping her foot. "You can sleep on the window-ledge but I will not let

you lie on my bed!" But
her father had followed
her up the stairs and
heard her cross words.

"It may seem hard, little
daughter," he said, "but
this Frog helped you
once and now it is your

turn to help him. You must do as he asks."

So the Princess put the Frog upon her silken pillow and he soon fell asleep but the Princess vowed she would remain awake all night.

She lay quiet and still beside him for a long while but after a time her eyelids began to droop and then she, too, nodded off.

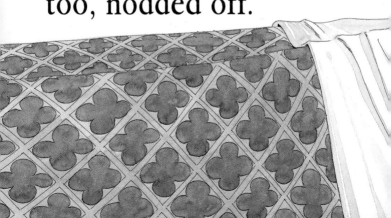

As the morning sunlight filled her room, the Frog awoke. Without a word, he hopped off the bed, down the stairs and was gone.

"Thank goodness," said the Princess. "Now I will never see him again." But she was greatly mistaken, for that night, as darkness fell, she heard a gentle tap at her door. A soft voice called out:

*"Open the door,
my Princess dear,
Open the door
to your true love here!
And remember the words
that you and I said,
by the fountain cool, in
the greenwood shade."*

With a sinking heart,
the Princess opened the
door and there squatted
the Frog. Once again he

wished to lie upon her
pillow and once again
the Princess had to do
as she was bid.

The following morning
he was gone again and
the Princess believed
that he was now gone
for good. But the Frog
returned again that night
and slept on her pillow
as before.

When the Princess awoke the next morning, she slowly opened her eyes, dreading the sight of the Frog beside her on the pillow. But gone was the ugly creature who had shared her room.

Instead she gazed into
the eyes of the most
handsome Prince she

had ever seen. He stood
by her bed and looked
down at her tenderly.

"Sweet Princess, you have saved me from a wicked spell," he said, gently taking her hand. "An evil witch turned me into a frog and told me I would remain for ever in the fountain pool.

The only way the spell could be broken would be if a Princess took me home and let me eat from her plate and sleep on her pillow. This you have done with great kindness.

The Princess blushed to think how unwillingly she had saved the Prince. He was so captivated by her beauty that he forgave her instantly and, bending on one knee, asked her to marry him.

She very readily agreed
and as they descended
the marble staircase, up
drove a splendid coach.

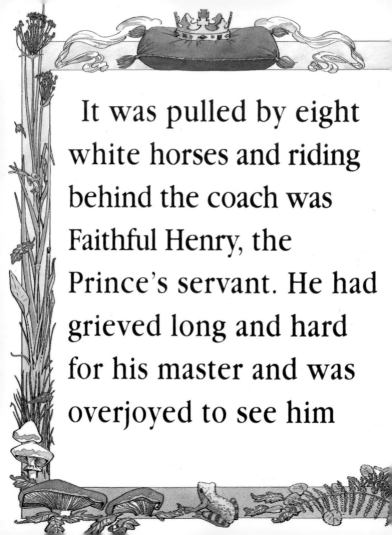

It was pulled by eight
white horses and riding
behind the coach was
Faithful Henry, the
Prince's servant. He had
grieved long and hard
for his master and was
overjoyed to see him

returned from the
witch's enchantment.

The Princess waved
farewell and, with much
merriment, set off with
her Prince for his
Kingdom where they
lived happily ever after.

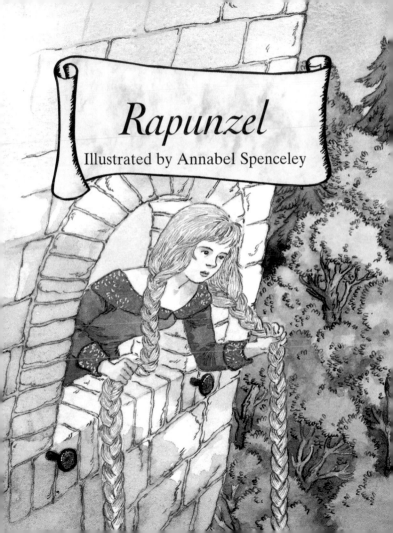

Rapunzel

Illustrated by Annabel Spenceley

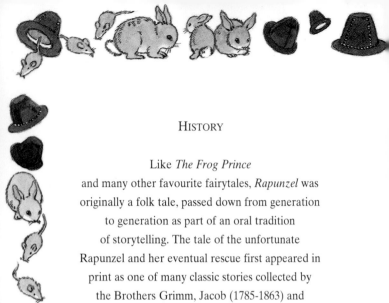

HISTORY

Like *The Frog Prince*
and many other favourite fairytales, *Rapunzel* was
originally a folk tale, passed down from generation
to generation as part of an oral tradition
of storytelling. The tale of the unfortunate
Rapunzel and her eventual rescue first appeared in
print as one of many classic stories collected by
the Brothers Grimm, Jacob (1785-1863) and
Wilhelm (1786-1859) It is now well loved throughout the world.

Once upon a time there lived a man and his wife. Sadly, they felt their lives were empty because they had no children. These good people lived in a little house and at the back of the house was a little window. From this window the man and his wife could see a lovely garden full of many beautiful flowers and fine vegetables.

But the garden was surrounded on all four sides by a high wall, and no-one dared enter, for it belonged to a powerful witch who was feared by all who lived near.

One day the woman stood at her window overlooking the garden and there she saw a bed full of the finest rampion. This was a wonderful herb and the leaves looked so fresh and

green that she longed to
eat them. Day by day,
her desire grew greater
and because she knew
she couldn't possibly
reach the tasty herb, she
pined away and became
quite pale and ill.

Then her husband grew worried.

"What is the matter, dear wife?" he asked.

"Oh," she answered, "if I don't get some of that lovely rampion to eat, I'm sure I shall die."

The man, who loved her dearly, sat down and wondered what he might do to help his ailing wife. After a time he said to himself, "Come! Rather than let my wife die I must fetch

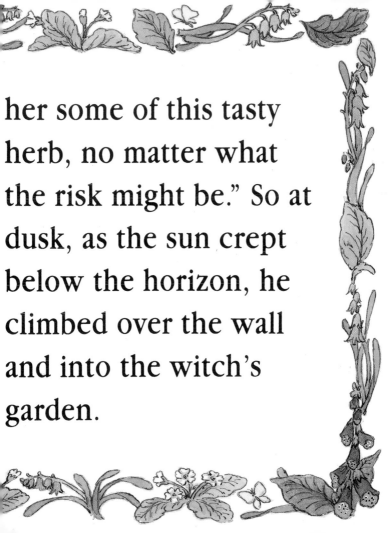

her some of this tasty
herb, no matter what
the risk might be." So at
dusk, as the sun crept
below the horizon, he
climbed over the wall
and into the witch's
garden.

Hastily he gathered a handful of leaves, all the while looking over his shoulder in case he should be seen. But no-one seemed to notice him there and soon he had returned to his wife.

She was well pleased
to see what he had
brought and soon made
a salad with the leaves
which tasted so good
that her spirits rose and
her good health
returned forthwith.

But after the herb had been eaten her longing for the forbidden food was greater than ever. Sadly she gazed from her little window and soon she grew ill once more. Once again her

husband asked her what
me might do to help.
"If you really want to
make me well again,"
his wife replied, "please
return to the garden
and fetch me more
rampion."

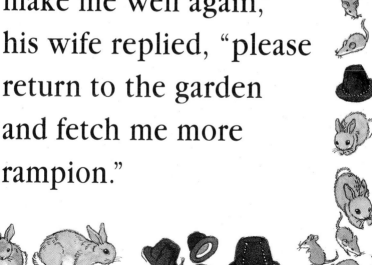

So at dusk, as dark shadows crept across the ground, over the wall he climbed — but when he reached the other side he drew back in terror for there before him was the old witch.

"How dare you climb into my garden and steal my rampion like a common thief?" she demanded angrily.

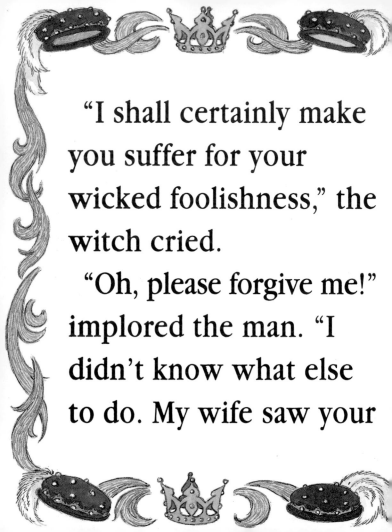

"I shall certainly make you suffer for your wicked foolishness," the witch cried.

"Oh, please forgive me!" implored the man. "I didn't know what else to do. My wife saw your

rampion from her
window, and it looked
so wonderful that she
longed to taste it.
Indeed, she believed
she would certainly
have died if her wish
had not been met."

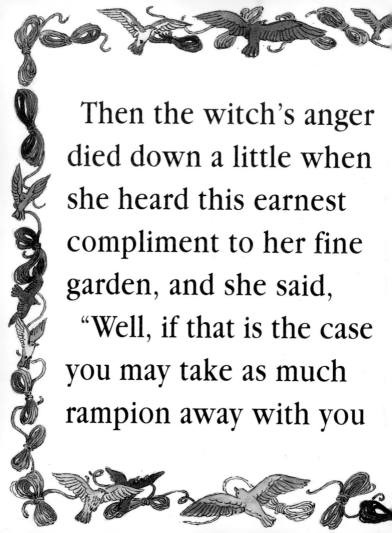

Then the witch's anger
died down a little when
she heard this earnest
compliment to her fine
garden, and she said,
"Well, if that is the case
you may take as much
rampion away with you

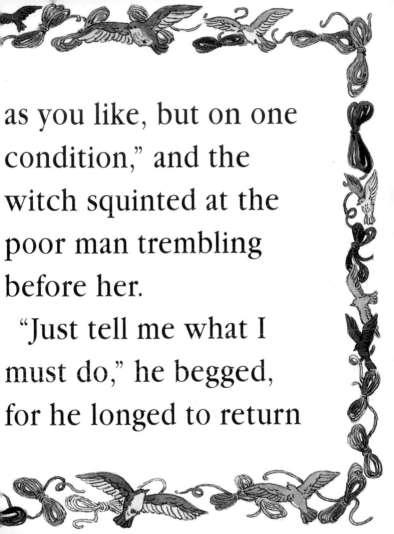

as you like, but on one condition," and the witch squinted at the poor man trembling before her.

"Just tell me what I must do," he begged, for he longed to return to his own safe home.

"You must give me the child which your wife will shortly bring into the world. I will raise it myself and look after it like a good mother," said the witch.

In his terror the man agreed to everything she asked, and he was then allowed to go free. Some time later his wife did indeed have a child. But as soon as the baby was born the witch

appeared by her cradle and carried her away. She named the child Rapunzel, which is another name for rampion, the herb which grew so well in her garden.

Rapunzel grew up to be the most beautiful child under the sun. Her eyes were as blue as harebells and her lovely long hair glinted like spun gold in the sunshine.

The witch wanted to be sure that no-one would ever find her, so when Rapunzel was twelve years old the wicked woman shut her up in a tower in the middle of a great wood.

The tower had neither stairs nor doors and the only window was high up, right at the very top.

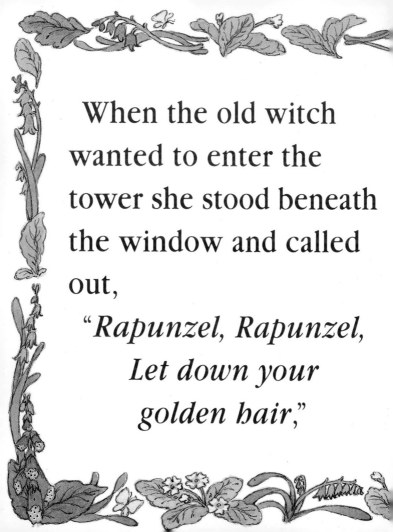

When the old witch
wanted to enter the
tower she stood beneath
the window and called
out,

"*Rapunzel, Rapunzel,*
Let down your
golden hair,"

for Rapunzel had the
most beautiful long hair,
and it was wonderfully
strong. Whenever she
heard the witch's voice
she unloosed her plaits,
and let her hair fall
down out of the window.

The golden tresses reached the ground far below, and then the old witch held on tight and climbed up.

So Rapunzel lived in her tall tower and the years slowly passed, but one day a Prince was riding through the wood and as he drew near the tower he heard someone singing so sweetly that he stood still as if spell-bound and listened. It was lonely young Rapunzel who had no other way to while away the hours than by letting her sweet voice ring out

into the wood. The
Prince longed to meet
the owner of such a
beautiful voice, but he
sought in vain for a
door in the tower and
so he rode back home,
greatly puzzled.

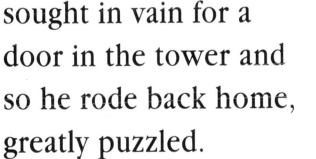

He was so haunted by
the sweet song that he
returned every day and
stood under the tower
to listen.

One day, when he was standing thus behind a tree, he saw the old witch approach the tower and call out,

"*Rapunzel, Rapunzel,*
Let down your
golden hair."

Then Rapunzel let
down her plaits, and
the witch climbed up.

"So that's the staircase, is it?" said the Prince to himself. "Then I too will climb it and try my luck." The following day at dusk, he went to the foot of the tower and cried out,

"Rapunzel, Rapunzel, Let down your golden hair." Down tumbled the golden tresses and in a trice the Prince had climbed right up to the top of the tower.

At first Rapunzel was terribly frightened to see him clamber over her windowsill, for she had never met a man before, but the Prince spoke to her kindly, and told her at once that his heart had been so touched by her singing that he felt he would have no peace of mind till he had seen her. Then Rapunzel forgot her fear, and when he asked her to marry him

she quickly agreed.
   "For," she said to
herself, "he is young
and handsome, and I'll
certainly be happier
with him than I would
ever be with the
wicked old witch."

So she put her hand in
his and said, "I will
gladly go with you, but
how am I to get down
from the tower?"

The Prince thought
hard and Rapunzel
thought hard and soon
she had the answer.
"You must come and
visit me every evening
for that is when the
witch leaves me on my

own. Bring a skein of silk thread with you each time and I will make a secret rope-ladder. When it is finished I will climb down, and then you shall carry me off on your horse."

And so he came to her every evening and she worked busily upon the ladder while the witch was away. But when she heard the old woman call for her she quickly hid it under her bed.

The old witch, of course, knew nothing of what was going on, till one day Rapunzel, half-asleep and not thinking of what she was saying, turned to the witch and asked

"How is it, good mother, that when I let down my hair you are so much harder to pull up than the young Prince? He always climbs up and is with me in a moment."

"Oh! You wicked child," cried the witch. "What is this I hear? I thought I had hidden you safely from the whole world, and now I hear you have managed to trick and deceive me!"

Angrily she seized Rapunzel's beautiful hair and wound it round her left hand. Then she grasped a pair of sharp scissors in her right hand and *snip snap*, cut off the long tresses.

There lay the beautiful plaits upon the ground. But this wasn't enough for the old witch and she took Rapunzel to a bleak and deserted spot far away, and there she left her to live in great

loneliness and misery.
Then the witch
returned to the tower
and that evening carefully
fastened Rapunzel's
plaits on to a hook
beside the window, and
waited for the Prince.

Sure enough, as the forest stilled and the sky grew dark he arrived at the bottom of the tower and called out,

"Rapunzel, Rapunzel, Let down your golden hair."

Then the witch let down the plaits and the Prince climbed up as usual, but instead of his beloved Rapunzel he found the old witch! She fixed her evil, glittering eyes upon him

and cried mockingly,
  "Aha! You thought to
find your lady love, but
the pretty bird has flown
away! She has lost her
song, for the cat caught
it, and will scratch out
your eyes, too!"

The old witch cackled. "Rapunzel is lost to you for ever — you will never see her again!"

The Prince was filled with grief and despair. He jumped right out of the window and landed in the rose bushes far below. There the sharp thorns in which he fell pierced his eyes.

His eyes were blinded and all alone he wandered through the wood. He would surely have starved but for the gifts of food that the friendly forest animals brought to him.

The little squirrels ceased chattering and raided the stores they had been busily hiding for winter. Gratefully he nibbled their sweet hazelnuts and chestnuts while they watched him

timidly from the trees.
The mice fetched
plump blackberries and
listened sorrowfully as
the poor Prince wept
and lamented the loss
of Rapunzel, his lovely
bride.

So he strayed through
the wilderness, as
wretched and unhappy
as any man could be.
The little birds sang to
him but their merry
voices could not
compare to that sweet

voice he had once
heard in the tall tower.

  But after many months
had passed he heard a
sound which brought
tears to his poor blind
eyes. Could it be his
Rapunzel singing?

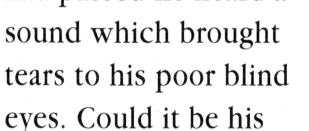

Sure enough, he had reached the desolate place where the poor girl lived all alone. Hurriedly he stumbled towards the singing and Rapunzel recognised her Prince immediately.

Happily she fell into
his arms and wept for
joy. But two of her tears
dropped on his eyes,
and in a moment they
became quite clear, and
he saw as well as he
had ever done.

Then he led her to his
kingdom, where they
were welcomed with
great joy, and soon
they were married and
lived happily ever after.